THE MIND'S APPETITE

AURELIE DUNCANSON

ACKNOWLEDGMENT

To my family, for your endless love and encouragement, you've been my greatest strength.

To my friends, who cheered me on even in moments of doubt.

To the incredible editors and mentors whose guidance shaped this story into what it is.

To my readers, you're the heart of every word written here.

And to every inspiration along the way, thank you for making this adventure possible.

TABLE OF CONTENTS

CHAPTER 1

A QUIET EVENING

Elizabeth adjusted the dining table one last time, her fingers lingering as she smoothed out a faint wrinkle in the linen cloth. The soft fabric felt cool beneath her touch, a stark contrast to the golden-hour light spilling into the room, bathing it in a *deceptive* warmth. To her, the glow felt *hollow*, a cruel imitation of life that only emphasized the *absence* she couldn't ignore. Every detail in the room was immaculate—gleaming silverware, porcelain plates perfectly aligned, fresh flowers standing proud in a crystal vase. Yet, the meticulousness of it all felt *futile*, an empty ritual to mask the silence.

The house loomed around her, its vastness pressing down with an almost *suffocating* weight. Every sound she made was magnified—the faint rustle of the cloth, the soft scrape of a chair being nudged into place, the delicate clink of a fork as she adjusted its position. These small noises reverberated through the space, each one a reminder of how *alone* she was. The stillness that followed was *unbearable*, broken only by the faint hum of the clock on the mantle, counting moments she *wished* she could escape.

Her eyes drifted toward the front door, a habit she hadn't yet broken. She *half-expected* it to swing open, for Luc to walk in with his easy, disarming smile, his presence filling the room with warmth no sunlight could replicate. But the door stayed shut, unmoving, and reality settled in once more like a *heavy fog*. Luc was *gone*. No footsteps would echo down the hall, no voice would call her name. The ache of his absence was *constant*, woven into the fabric of the life she now lived alone.

It had been six months since the accident. Six months of stumbling through days that felt *too long* and nights that felt *unbearably empty*. The grief wasn't just a weight pressing on her shoulders; it was an *unwelcome companion* that shadowed her every move, invading her thoughts and stealing her breath at the most *unexpected* moments. She had thought tonight might be different. Inviting friends over for dinner was supposed to be a *step forward*, an attempt to reclaim a piece of her old self. Yet, as she folded the last napkin and adjusted the silverware, a *chill* crept up her spine. It was as though the house itself *resented* her efforts, the quiet rooms whispering that it was *too soon*, that she wasn't ready.

The silence was interrupted by the distant chime of the clock in the hallway, its rhythmic toll announcing the approach of seven. Elizabeth glanced at her phone on the countertop. There were no new messages from Samuel. Her son had gone to stay with a friend for the weekend—a *much-needed respite* for both of them. He had been distant lately, retreating further into his world of gaming, music, and late-night texts with friends. She knew he was grieving too, in his own way, but it felt like they were on *parallel tracks*, unable to meet. Elizabeth couldn't blame him. How could she, when she didn't even know how to be *enough* for herself anymore?

Returning to the kitchen, she opened the oven to check on the roast. The aroma of rosemary and garlic filled the air, comforting yet *bittersweet*. Cooking had once been a joy, something she and Luc had shared. Now, it felt *mechanical*, like going through the motions of a life that no longer fit. She adjusted the temperature slightly and closed the oven door with a soft click.

Her thoughts wandered as she set out the wine glasses on the table. She could almost hear Luc's laugh, low and rich, teasing her about the meticulous way she arranged everything. *"You could open a five-star restaurant with how you're setting this up, Lizzie,"* he would have said. The memory brought a faint smile to her lips before reality swept it away.

The house had always been *too large* for just the three of them, but Luc's presence had filled the empty corners with life. Now, every room felt *cavernous*, the high ceilings and expansive hallways echoing with a silence she couldn't escape. She had tried to downsize, but Samuel had resisted. This was the only home he had ever known, and despite the painful memories, Elizabeth couldn't bring herself to force the change.

She moved to the living room, where she had already tidied the cushions and dusted the shelves. The fireplace, once a centerpiece of their family evenings, was clean and unused, its grate *cold and unwelcoming*. On the mantelpiece, a photo of Luc and Samuel caught her eye. It was from a camping trip two summers ago. Luc's arm was slung around their son's shoulders, both of them grinning at the camera, their faces sunburned and carefree. Elizabeth felt her throat tighten as she reached out to adjust the frame, her fingertips brushing against the glass.

The faint buzz of the refrigerator hummed in the background, a low, persistent reminder of the stillness that had taken over their lives. She inhaled deeply, steadying herself for the evening ahead, trying to ignore the persistent ache in her chest that whispered she might never truly heal.

Back in the dining room, she lit the candles in the center of the table, their soft glow adding a touch of warmth to the otherwise *sterile* atmosphere. The flickering flames danced in the dim light, casting shadows on the walls. For a moment, she simply stood there, watching the interplay of light and shadow, her mind drifting to places she didn't want to go.

A faint creak from the hallway broke her reverie. Her head snapped toward the sound, her heart quickening. *"Samuel?"* she called out, her voice tentative, knowing full well he wasn't home. There was no response. She shook her head, a wry smile tugging at her lips. *"It's just the house settling,"* she murmured to herself, though the explanation did little to calm her nerves.

She busied herself with arranging the flowers on the sideboard, adjusting the stems until the bouquet looked just right. The lilies were a *stark white*, their delicate petals contrasting with the dark wood of the vase. They were Luc's favorite, a fact that had slipped her mind when she bought them. Now, they felt like an *unintentional tribute*, their presence both comforting and haunting.

As she stepped back to admire her work, her gaze was drawn to the large bay window that overlooked the garden. The sun had dipped below the horizon, and the twilight cast a *deep blue hue* over the scene. The shadows of the trees swayed gently in the breeze, their movements hypnotic. For a moment, she thought she saw a figure among them, a tall silhouette standing still amidst the rustling leaves. Her breath hitched, and she moved closer to the glass, her eyes straining to make out the shape. But when she blinked, the figure was gone, leaving only the familiar outline of the garden shed and the empty swing set.

Elizabeth pressed a hand to her chest, her heartbeat erratic. *"It's just your imagination,"* she whispered, but the unease lingered. She drew the curtains closed, shutting out the night and the creeping sense of vulnerability it brought.

In the kitchen, she retrieved the dessert from the fridge, a carefully crafted tart that had taken her all afternoon to prepare. She set it on the counter and stared at it for a long moment. Luc would have teased her for going to so much trouble. *"Store-bought would've been fine,"* he'd say with a wink, though he always ate every bite of her creations with relish. The memory brought a pang of longing so sharp it left her breathless.

She leaned against the counter, her hands gripping the edge as she tried to steady herself. The weight of the evening ahead pressed down on her, the pressure to appear *composed and capable* when all she wanted to do was crumble. She had promised herself that tonight would be a *step forward*, a chance to reconnect with the world beyond her grief. But now, standing alone in the quiet kitchen, she wasn't sure she had the strength.

The clock chimed again, its sound a jarring reminder of the time. Elizabeth straightened, forcing herself to move. She arranged the tart on a serving platter, adding a garnish of fresh berries for a touch of color. The action was automatic, her hands moving with a precision born of habit. But her mind was elsewhere, lost in the *labyrinth of memories* and what-ifs that haunted her.

She carried the platter to the dining table and set it down gently, adjusting its position until it was perfectly centered. Her gaze lingered on the empty chair at the head of the table, the place where Luc had always sat. The emptiness seemed to mock her, a stark reminder of everything she had lost. She turned away quickly, her throat tight.

Elizabeth moved to the front hallway, checking her reflection in the mirror by the door. She smoothed her hair and adjusted the neckline of her blouse, trying to convince herself that she looked put together. But the woman staring back at her looked *tired*, her eyes shadowed with exhaustion and sorrow. She pressed her lips together and straightened her shoulders, willing herself to believe in the *illusion of control*.

The house was ready. Every detail had been attended to, every surface cleaned and polished, every corner free of dust. But as Elizabeth stood in the quiet, her hands clasped tightly in front of her, she couldn't shake the feeling that it was all for *nothing*. The emptiness remained, a void that no amount of preparation could fill.

She glanced at the clock one final time. The guests would arrive soon, their laughter and conversation filling the void, if only temporarily. Elizabeth took a deep breath and closed her eyes, bracing herself for the evening ahead. For now, she had done all she could. And yet, as the silence stretched around her, she couldn't help but feel that the house—and her life—was still *unbearably empty*.

CHAPTER 2

FAMILIAR FACES, UNEASY CONNECTIONS

Elizabeth's pulse quickened as the doorbell rang, a sharp sound that broke through the heavy silence of the house. She glanced at her reflection in the hallway mirror one last time, smoothing her blouse with trembling hands. Her breath hitched as she moved toward the door, her heels clicking softly against the polished wood floor.

When she opened it, Marc stood there, a warm smile softening his angular features.

"Elizabeth," he greeted, his voice steady and calm, the kind of tone that seemed to ground her even in her most chaotic moments.

"Marc," she said, relief flooding her voice. *"You're the first to arrive."*

He stepped inside, his presence immediately filling the space with a quiet reassurance. He carried a bottle of wine in one hand and a bouquet of daisies in the other. *"I wasn't sure what you'd prefer, so I brought both."*

Elizabeth took the flowers, their cheerful yellow petals a stark contrast to the lingering gray in her heart. *"Thank you. These are lovely."* She gestured toward the dining room. *"Please, make yourself comfortable. Dinner will be ready soon."*

Marc moved with an ease that felt almost out of place in the house. He set the wine on the table and took in the room with a quick but appreciative glance. *"It looks beautiful, Elizabeth. You've outdone yourself."*

She smiled faintly, the compliment a balm against her nervousness. *"It's nothing, really. Just a small gathering."*

"Small gatherings often mean the most," he replied, his voice gentle.

Before she could respond, the doorbell chimed again. Her stomach tightened as she excused herself to answer it. This time, it was Paul. His presence felt heavier, less comforting than Marc's. He carried himself with an air of quiet intensity, his sharp eyes scanning her face as though searching for something unspoken.

"Paul," Elizabeth said, her voice betraying a hint of hesitation. *"I'm glad you could make it."*

"Wouldn't miss it," he replied, his tone neutral but his gaze lingering a moment too long. He stepped inside, his movements deliberate. As he entered the dining room, his eyes locked briefly with Marc's. The air between them shifted, charged with an unspoken tension. Elizabeth noticed it immediately, her nerves prickling.

"Paul," Marc greeted with a polite nod, his expression unreadable.

"Marc," Paul replied, his tone clipped. The two men exchanged a look that seemed to carry the weight of a shared history, though neither elaborated. Elizabeth's unease deepened, but she pushed it aside, focusing instead on arranging the flowers Marc had brought.

The doorbell rang once more, and Elizabeth hurried to answer it. This time, it was Claire and Chloé, their laughter spilling into the hallway before she even opened the door fully. The sight of them brought a wave of bittersweet nostalgia.

"Elizabeth!" Claire exclaimed, pulling her into a tight embrace. *"It's been too long."*

"Far too long," Chloé agreed, her smile warm but her eyes shadowed with something Elizabeth couldn't quite place.

"I'm so glad you both could come," Elizabeth said, her voice wavering slightly as she stepped back to let them in.

The two women entered, their energy a welcome contrast to the tension that had settled in the dining room. Claire's auburn curls bounced as she moved, her presence vibrant and commanding. Chloé, quieter but no less engaging, carried a small box of pastries, which she handed to Elizabeth with a shy smile.

"Just a little something for dessert," Chloé said.

"Thank you," Elizabeth replied, touched by the gesture. *"They look wonderful."*

As the women joined the men in the dining room, Elizabeth lingered in the kitchen for a moment, steadying herself. The soft hum of conversation drifted toward her, punctuated by occasional laughter. It should have been comforting, but instead, it felt like a reminder of how much had changed.

When she finally rejoined the group, the atmosphere had settled into a tentative rhythm. Marc and Claire were discussing a recent art exhibit, their tones light and engaging. Chloé listened intently, occasionally chiming in with her own observations. Paul, however, remained quiet, his gaze darting between the others with a calculating intensity that set Elizabeth on edge.

Dinner was served, and the group moved to the table. The meal began with polite conversation, the clinking of silverware filling the pauses. Elizabeth tried to focus on the flow of the evening, but her mind kept drifting. Every now and then, her eyes would settle on Marc, and for a fleeting moment, she would see Luc. It wasn't just his dark hair or the way his smile crinkled at the corners of his eyes. It was something deeper, a quiet confidence that reminded her so much of her late husband that it made her chest ache.

"Elizabeth," Claire said, pulling her from her thoughts. *"This roast is incredible. You've outdone yourself."*

"Thank you," Elizabeth replied, her voice soft. *"I'm glad you're enjoying it."*

"It's been ages since we've all been together like this," Chloé added, her tone wistful. *"I've missed it."*

"We all have," Marc agreed, his gaze briefly meeting Elizabeth's. There was something in his expression—a quiet understanding that made her feel seen in a way she hadn't in months.

The conversation turned to memories of Luc, and Elizabeth felt her composure begin to slip. Claire didn't know Liz really- She is a mental institute patient. Paul, who had been mostly silent, added a comment about Luc's knack for diffusing tense situations. His voice was steady, but there was a flicker of something in his eyes—regret, perhaps, or guilt. Elizabeth couldn't tell.

"He was one of a kind," Marc said, his voice soft but firm.

Elizabeth's throat tightened. She looked down at her plate, her appetite gone. The weight of their words pressed down on her, each memory a sharp reminder of what she had lost. She tried to focus on the flickering candlelight, on the warmth of the room, but the grief was relentless, seeping into every corner of her mind.

"Elizabeth?" Chloé's voice was gentle, her concern evident. *"Are you okay?"*

Elizabeth forced a smile, though it felt brittle. *"I'm fine,"* she said, her voice barely above a whisper. *"Just... a lot of memories tonight."*

"That's natural," Claire said, reaching across the table to squeeze her hand. *"We're here for you."*

The sincerity in her friend's voice was both comforting and overwhelming. Elizabeth nodded, unable to trust herself to speak.

As the meal progressed, the conversation shifted to lighter topics, but Elizabeth found it increasingly difficult to stay present. Her gaze kept returning to Marc, her mind playing cruel tricks on her. At one point, she could have sworn she saw Luc sitting across from her, his familiar smile lighting up his face. She blinked, and the image dissolved, leaving only Marc, who was watching her with quiet concern.

"Elizabeth," he said softly, his voice cutting through the fog of her thoughts. *"Are you sure you're all right?"*

"I'm fine," she said quickly, though her voice wavered. She picked up her wine glass, hoping the sip would steady her.

The evening wore on, the guests lingering at the table. The warmth of the wine and the glow of the candles created an intimate atmosphere, but Elizabeth couldn't shake the unease that had settled over her. The tension between Paul and Marc remained palpable, an undercurrent that no one addressed but everyone seemed to sense.

As the conversation ebbed and flowed, Elizabeth found herself drifting again. The shadows cast by the candlelight seemed to dance on the walls, their movements almost hypnotic. She stared at the empty chair at the head of the table, where Luc would have sat, his presence a steady anchor in their lives. The ache in her chest deepened, a hollow void that no amount of company could fill.

And then, she saw him.

Across the table, where Marc had been sitting moments ago, Luc's face stared back at her. His dark eyes held hers, filled with the warmth and love she had missed so desperately. Her breath caught, her heart pounding in her chest. For a moment, everything else faded away—the voices, the candlelight, the weight of her grief. It was just him, looking at her as though he had never left.

"Luc?" she whispered, the word slipping out before she could stop it.

"Elizabeth?" Marc 's voice broke through the illusion, and she blinked, the image shattering. It was him, not Luc, sitting across from her, his expression filled with concern.

"I'm sorry," she said quickly, her voice trembling. *"I—I thought..."* She trailed off, unable to finish the sentence. The room felt stifling, the air too thick to breathe.

Marc reached out, his hand brushing hers lightly. *"It's okay,"* he said gently. *"You've been through so much. It's understandable."*

Elizabeth nodded, though her mind was racing. She felt the eyes of the others on her, their concern palpable. She forced a smile, trying to regain her composure. *"I think I just need some fresh air,"* she said, pushing her chair back and standing.

As she stepped out onto the back patio, the cool night air enveloped her, a stark contrast to the warmth of the dining room. She leaned against the railing, her hands gripping the wood tightly as she tried to steady herself. The stars above seemed impossibly far away, their light faint and distant. She closed her eyes, willing the image of Luc to fade, but it lingered, a ghost of a memory she couldn't escape.

CHAPTER 3

FAMILIARITY
BREEDS CONTEMPT

Elizabeth tightened her grip on the stem of her wineglass, the coolness of the glass grounding her, if only for a moment. The room was filled with the hum of conversation, but it all felt distant, like the muffled echoes of a dream. She forced herself to smile as Chloé recounted a story about her latest trip to Paris, her hands gesturing animatedly. Claire laughed in response, her voice lilting, but Elizabeth barely heard the words. Her focus kept drifting to Marc.

He sat across the table, his posture relaxed, his face illuminated by the flickering candlelight. Something about the way he held his glass—the tilt of his wrist, the way his fingers curled around the stem—sent a chill down her spine. It was uncanny. The gesture was so familiar, so achingly reminiscent of Luc, that for a moment, she couldn't breathe. Her chest tightened, and she had to look away, her gaze darting to the bouquet of lilies in the center of the table. The flowers seemed to mock her, their pristine petals a stark reminder of what she had lost.

"Elizabeth," Claire's voice cut through her thoughts, sharp and probing. "How are you really doing?"

The question hung in the air, heavy and unavoidable. Elizabeth's fingers tightened around her glass, her knuckles whitening. She opened her mouth to respond, but the words caught in her throat. She could feel all their eyes on her, waiting, expecting. The warmth of the wine in her hand felt suddenly oppressive, its scent too strong.

"I…" she began, her voice faltering. "I'm managing. It's… a process."

Claire leaned forward, her expression soft but insistent. "It's okay to admit that it's hard. You don't have to pretend for us."

Elizabeth's stomach churned. Pretend. The word felt like an accusation, though she knew Claire meant well. She glanced at Marc, hoping for a distraction, but his gaze was already on her, calm and steady. It was the kind of look Luc used to give her when he sensed she was struggling, a silent reassurance that he was there, that she wasn't alone. Her chest ached, the lines between memory and reality blurring.

"I'm not pretending," Elizabeth said, her voice sharper than she intended. She saw Claire flinch slightly, and guilt immediately followed. "I mean… I'm trying. That's all I can do right now."

Chloé reached out, her warm hand resting lightly on Elizabeth's arm. "We're here for you, Lizzie. Always."

Elizabeth nodded, but the words felt hollow. The room seemed to close in around her, the walls pressing closer, the air growing heavier. She took a sip of her wine, the liquid bitter on her tongue. Her eyes drifted back to Marc, who was laughing softly at something Paul had said. The sound sent a shiver through her. It wasn't just similar to Luc's laugh; it was identical. The same low, rich timbre, the same way it lingered in the air, warm and inviting.

"You're staring again," Claire's voice cut in, teasing but pointed. Elizabeth's head snapped toward her, heat rushing to her cheeks.

"I wasn't…" she started, but the words faltered. Claire raised an eyebrow, a small smirk playing on her lips.

"It's okay, Lizzie. Marc 's a catch. If you're ready to… you know, dip your toes back in the water, there's no shame in that."

Elizabeth's stomach twisted. "That's not… I wasn't…" She trailed off, her hands trembling slightly as she set her glass down. The clink of the glass against the table was louder than she intended, drawing everyone's attention. She forced a laugh, trying to mask her discomfort. "I was just lost in thought."

Paul's gaze lingered on her for a moment longer than necessary, his expression unreadable. There was something about him that unsettled her, though she couldn't quite put her finger on it. He and Marc exchanged a glance, a fleeting look that seemed to carry weight, though Elizabeth couldn't decipher its meaning. She felt a pang of paranoia, her mind racing with possibilities. Were they talking about her? Judging her? Or was it something else entirely?

"Loss changes you," Claire said, her tone softer now. "It's not about replacing anyone, but finding a way to live again. Don't you think?"

Elizabeth's breath hitched. The question felt like a trap, its edges sharp and unforgiving. She glanced at Marc again, her mind betraying her with flashes of Luc's face. The way he used to look at her, the way his eyes crinkled at the corners when he smiled. She blinked rapidly, trying to dispel the images, but they clung to her like cobwebs.

"I don't know," she said finally, her voice barely above a whisper. "I don't know what living again even looks like."

The table fell silent, the weight of her words settling over them like a heavy blanket. Elizabeth felt exposed, her vulnerability laid bare. She hated it, the way they looked at her with pity in their eyes. She wanted to scream, to tell them to stop, but the words wouldn't come.

Marc cleared his throat, breaking the silence. "Everyone grieves differently," he said, his voice steady and reassuring. "There's no right or wrong way to do it."

Elizabeth's eyes flicked to him, and for a moment, she saw Luc. Not just in his gestures or his voice, but in the way he carried himself, the quiet strength that radiated from him. Her heart clenched, the ache of loss threatening to consume her. She looked away quickly, focusing on the flickering candlelight.

The rest of the dinner passed in a haze. Elizabeth picked at her food, barely tasting it, her mind a whirlwind of emotions. She laughed when she was supposed to, nodded at the right moments, but it all felt hollow. Her gaze kept drifting back to Marc, each glance a fresh wound. She tried to focus on the conversation, but the words blurred together, their meaning lost.

"Lizzie," Chloé said suddenly, pulling her back to the present. "Do you remember that summer you told me about? The one where you and Luc went to the lake?"

Elizabeth froze, her fork hovering mid-air. The memory rushed back unbidden, vivid and painful. She could see it so clearly—the sun glinting off the water, Luc's laughter ringing out as he splashed her, the way he had looked at her, his eyes filled with love. Her throat tightened, and she set her fork down, unable to eat another bite.

"I remember," she said softly, her voice thick with emotion. She glanced at Marc, half-expecting him to chime in, to share a memory of his own. But he remained silent, his expression unreadable.

"You were so happy then," Claire said, her voice tinged with nostalgia. "I think Luc brought out the best in all of us."

Elizabeth's chest constricted, the pain almost physical. She wanted to tell them to stop, to change the subject, but she couldn't find the words. Her gaze drifted to Marc again, and for a moment, she thought she saw Luc staring back at her. Her breath caught, her vision swimming. She blinked rapidly, and the image was gone, replaced by Marc 's concerned face.

"Lizzie, are you okay?" Chloé asked, her voice laced with worry.

"I'm fine," Elizabeth said quickly, forcing a smile. "Just… tired, I think."

But she wasn't fine. The room felt stifling, the walls closing in around her. She could feel her grip on reality slipping, the lines between past and present blurring. She closed her eyes, taking a deep breath, but the memories wouldn't stop. Luc's voice echoed in her mind, soft and familiar.

"Lizzie," it whispered, sending a shiver down her spine. Her eyes snapped open, her heart pounding. She looked around the table, but no one else seemed to have heard it. Marc was speaking now, his voice calm and measured, but all Elizabeth could hear was Luc. She pressed a hand to her chest, her breath coming in shallow gasps.

"Excuse me," she said abruptly, pushing her chair back and standing. The sudden movement drew everyone's attention, their gazes following her as she hurried out of the room. She could hear their murmured voices behind her, but she didn't stop. She needed air, needed space.

In the hallway, she leaned against the wall, her hands trembling. She closed her eyes, trying to steady herself, but the whispers persisted. Luc's voice, soft and insistent, calling her name. She covered her ears, but it did little to block out the sound. Tears pricked at her eyes, and she pressed her forehead against the cool surface of the wall, willing herself to calm down.

"Elizabeth."

The voice was louder now, closer. Her eyes snapped open, and she turned sharply, her heart racing. Marc stood at the end of the hallway, his expression concerned. But for a split second, she saw Luc. His face, his eyes, his smile. Her breath caught, her vision swimming. She blinked, and the image dissolved, leaving only Marc standing there, his brow furrowed in concern.

"Are you sure you're okay?" he asked, his voice gentle but probing.

Elizabeth nodded quickly, wiping at her eyes. "I'm fine," she lied, her voice trembling. "Just… overwhelmed."

Marc took a cautious step closer, his gaze searching hers. "You don't have to do this alone, you know."

The words struck a chord, their familiarity cutting deep. They were words Luc had said to her once, in a moment of vulnerability. Her chest tightened, and she looked away, unable to meet Marc 's eyes.

"I just need a moment," she said, her voice barely above a whisper.

Marc hesitated, then nodded. "Take your time. We'll be here."

As he turned and walked away, Elizabeth felt a fresh wave of guilt wash over her. She pressed a hand to her chest, her heart pounding. The whispers had stopped, but the weight of her grief remained, heavy and suffocating. She closed her eyes, trying to steady her breathing, but the image of Luc's face lingered in her mind, haunting and inescapable.

CHAPTER 4

ECHOES OF THE PAST

Elizabeth sat in the dim light of her living room, the wineglass trembling slightly in her hand. The evening had left her *raw*, her nerves *frayed and exposed*. The shadows cast by the flickering candle on the coffee table seemed *alive*, shifting and stretching like they had secrets to tell. She closed her eyes, leaning back into the plush cushions, but the memories came rushing in, *unbidden and relentless*.

Luc's laugh echoed in her mind, *warm and rich*, as vivid as if he were sitting beside her. She could see him, the way his eyes crinkled at the corners when he smiled, the way his hand would rest on her knee during quiet moments. The room felt *colder without him*, the emptiness a tangible weight pressing against her chest. She opened her eyes, her breath hitching, and stared at the glass in her hand. The reflection of the candlelight danced across the wine's surface, reminding her of the way the sun had glinted off the lake that summer. The memory was *so sharp, so real*, that she could almost feel the warmth on her skin.

Claire sat across from Elizabeth, her eyes searching her face for any signs of the turmoil she knew her friend was hiding. The silence between them stretched uncomfortably, thick with unspoken words. Elizabeth avoided her gaze, tracing the rim of her coffee cup as if it could offer some comfort.

"Elizabeth," Claire's voice was soft but firm, the weight of concern evident. *"Are you okay? You've been so distant lately."*

Elizabeth's eyes flickered up briefly before dropping back to her cup. *"I'm fine,"* she said, the words feeling hollow even to her own ears. *"Just tired."*

Claire leaned forward, her expression sharpening. *"You keep saying that, but I know you're not fine. You're isolating yourself, Lizzie. This isn't like you."*

Elizabeth's jaw tightened, but she didn't respond immediately. Her fingers curled around the cup, the warmth doing little to soothe the cold knot in her chest. *"I'm not isolating,"* she muttered, trying to sound convincing. *"I hosted dinner, didn't I?*

Claire raised an eyebrow, not buying it. *"And spent half the evening staring at Marc like he was a ghost. You can't keep pretending everything's okay when it's clearly not."*

The words stung more than Elizabeth expected, and she shifted uncomfortably in her seat. *"I'm handling it in my own way,"* she said, her voice quieter now, almost defeated.

Claire's gaze softened, but there was still a trace of frustration in her eyes. *"I'm not trying to make you feel worse, Lizzie. I just... I'm worried. We all are."*

Elizabeth closed her eyes, feeling the weight of her friend's concern settle on her shoulders. She didn't want to admit it, but it was becoming harder to keep up the facade. *"I appreciate it,"* she whispered, *"but I need to do this on my own."*

There was a long pause before Claire spoke again, her voice gentle but insistent. *"Just promise me you'll talk to someone. You don't have to go through this alone."*

Elizabeth's chest tightened at the suggestion, but she forced a smile, though it didn't reach her eyes. *"I'll think about it,"* she said, knowing she wouldn't. She looked away, the conversation over before it could go any deeper.

The silence of the room enveloped her once again, *oppressive and unyielding.*

The memories crept back in, *insidious and inescapable.* She could see Luc standing in the doorway, his smile lighting up the room. She could hear his voice, *low and comforting,* as he read aloud from her favorite book. Tears pricked at her eyes, and she blinked them away, refusing to let them fall. But the harder she tried to push the memories away, the more *vivid* they became, until she wasn't sure where the past ended and the present began.

Her thoughts drifted to Marc, his *familiar gestures and mannerisms*. The way he had looked at her during dinner, his gaze *steady and unyielding*. It wasn't just his resemblance to Luc that unsettled her; it was the way he seemed to *see right through her*, as if he knew her deepest fears and regrets. And then there was Paul, with his cryptic glances and unreadable expressions. Something about him felt *off*, though she couldn't pinpoint why.

The room seemed to shift around her, the shadows growing *darker, more oppressive*. Elizabeth's breathing quickened, her chest tightening. She set the wineglass down and pressed her hands to her temples, trying to ground herself. But the whispers started, *soft and insistent*, like a distant voice carried on the wind.

"Lizzie."

Her head snapped up, her heart pounding. The room was empty, the shadows still. She shook her head, trying to dispel the lingering echo of Luc's voice. *It wasn't real. It couldn't be real.* But the doubt lingered, gnawing at the edges of her sanity.

The whispers grew louder, more *distinct*. They weren't just in her mind anymore; they were *all around her*, filling the room. She stumbled to her feet, her legs unsteady, and turned in a slow circle, her eyes darting to every corner.

"Who's there?" she demanded, her voice trembling.

Silence. And then, faintly, the sound of *footsteps*. Her breath hitched, and she backed toward the wall, her pulse racing.

"Luc?" she whispered, the name slipping out before she could stop it. The footsteps stopped, and for a moment, the room was still. Then, out of the corner of her eye, she saw a figure in the doorway. She turned sharply, her heart in her throat, but it was Marc.

"Elizabeth," he said softly, his expression unreadable. "Are you okay?"

She stared at him, her mind racing. For a moment, she wasn't sure if it was Marc or Luc standing there. The resemblance was *too strong*, the lines between memory and reality blurring once again. She pressed a hand to her chest, trying to steady her breathing.

"I… I thought I was alone," she said finally, her voice barely above a whisper.

Marc stepped into the room, his movements *slow and deliberate*. "I wanted to check on you. You seemed… upset earlier."

Elizabeth's gaze flicked to the shadows on the wall, her mind racing. "I'm fine," she said quickly, the lie feeling like a *shield*. "Just tired."

Marc 's eyes lingered on her, and she felt *exposed*, as if he could see every crack in her facade. "You don't have to pretend with me," he said gently. "I know how hard this is for you."

Her chest tightened, the weight of his words pressing down on her. She wanted to believe him, wanted to let herself be *vulnerable*, but the fear of breaking completely held her back.

"What do you want, Marc?" she asked, her voice sharper than she intended.

Marc hesitated, his expression unreadable. "I just want to help," he said finally. "That's all."

Elizabeth's mind raced, suspicion creeping in. There was something about him, about the way he spoke and the way he looked at her, that felt *off*. She couldn't shake the feeling that there was more to his presence than he was letting on. And then there was Paul, with his cryptic glances and vague comments. The two of them seemed connected, but *how?* And *why did they seem so familiar?*

The room felt stifling, the air heavy with *unspoken truths*. Elizabeth took a step back, her gaze fixed on Marc. "I think you should go," she said quietly, her voice trembling.

Marc 's brow furrowed, but he nodded. "If that's what you want," he said, his tone careful. He turned and walked to the doorway, but before he left, he paused, glancing back at her. "If you ever need someone to talk to, I'm here."

Elizabeth didn't respond, her gaze fixed on the shadows as he disappeared down the hallway. The silence that followed was *deafening*, the weight of the evening pressing down on her. She sank back onto the couch, her hands trembling. The whispers had stopped, but the *unease remained*, a constant presence in the back of her mind.

She closed her eyes, her thoughts *spiraling*. The memories of Luc were *relentless*, vivid and consuming. She could see him so clearly, hear his voice, feel his touch. It was as if he were still there, just out of reach. The line between reality and memory blurred further, her mind folding under the weight of her grief.

And then, she heard it again.

"Lizzie."

Her eyes snapped open, her heart pounding. She turned sharply, her gaze darting around the room. The shadows seemed to shift, and for a moment, she thought she saw him. *Luc, standing in the doorway, his smile warm and familiar.* Tears welled in her eyes, and she stumbled to her feet, reaching out.

"Luc?" she whispered, her voice trembling. The figure stepped closer, and her breath caught. But as he moved into the light, the illusion shattered. It wasn't Luc. It was Marc.

Her chest tightened, the weight of her grief threatening to consume her. She pressed a hand to her mouth, her tears spilling over. "I… I thought you were…"

Marc 's expression softened, and he took a cautious step closer. "Elizabeth," he said gently, his voice steady. "You're not alone in this. I'm here for you."

But in her mind, it wasn't Marc speaking. *It was Luc.* His voice, his words, his presence. She closed her eyes, letting the illusion take over, the lines between past and present blurring completely.

"I miss you," she whispered, her voice breaking. "I don't know how to do this without you."

Marc reached out, his hand resting lightly on her shoulder. "You don't have to," he said softly. "I'll help you through this."

Elizabeth's breath hitched, her heart aching. For a moment, she let herself believe it was Luc standing there, his touch grounding her, his words comforting. But as she opened her eyes, the illusion shattered once again, leaving only Marc. The realization hit her like a wave, the weight of her grief crashing down around her.

She pulled away, her hands trembling. "I can't... I can't do this," she said, her voice barely above a whisper. She turned and fled the room, the sound of her footsteps echoing in the silence. But even as she ran, she couldn't escape the whispers, the memories, the *haunting presence of Luc.* They were a part of her now, *inescapable and consuming,* the echoes of the past refusing to let her go.

CHAPTER 5

CONVERSATIONS IN THE SHADOWS

Elizabeth's hands trembled as she stood at the edge of the garden, the cool night air brushing against her skin. The voices from the dining room drifted faintly through the open French doors, fragmented and indistinct. She clenched her fists, trying to ground herself, but the unease coiling in her chest refused to dissipate. *Tonight felt different*—charged, as if the air itself carried secrets waiting to be uncovered.

She turned her gaze to the silhouettes moving inside. Paul's laughter rang out, low and smooth, mingling with Claire's soft murmur. Elizabeth's stomach churned. She couldn't shake the feeling that Paul's presence was *more than coincidence*. He'd been too attentive, too knowing, as though he'd been watching her *long before tonight*.

"Elizabeth?"

She spun around, startled. Claire stood behind her, a shawl draped over her shoulders, concern etched on her face.

"Are you okay?" Claire asked, her voice gentle but probing.

Elizabeth forced a smile, though it felt brittle. "I needed some air. That's all."

Claire stepped closer, her eyes searching Elizabeth's face. "You've been distant all night. *We're worried about you.*"

"*We?*" Elizabeth's voice sharpened despite herself. She regretted it instantly when Claire's expression faltered.

"Me, Chloé, Marc. Even Paul. *We all care about you, Lizzie.* You've been through so much, and it's okay to lean on us."

Elizabeth's chest tightened. The way Claire spoke, so carefully, so deliberately, felt *rehearsed.* It wasn't just concern; it was *something else. Something calculated.*

"I appreciate it," Elizabeth said, her tone clipped. She turned back toward the garden, hoping Claire would take the hint and leave. Instead, Claire's hand rested lightly on her arm.

"Luc wouldn't want you to shut us out," Claire said softly.

Elizabeth froze. The mention of his name felt like a slap, *sharp and stinging.* She turned to Claire, her eyes blazing. "*Don't.*"

Claire's lips parted, but whatever she was about to say was cut off by the sound of footsteps. Paul emerged from the shadows, his tall frame illuminated by the soft glow of the garden lights. His presence felt *intrusive,* as though he'd been eavesdropping.

"Am I interrupting?" he asked, his voice smooth and unbothered.

Elizabeth's gaze flicked to Claire, who hesitated before stepping back. "I'll give you two a moment," Claire said, retreating toward the house.

Paul's eyes lingered on Elizabeth, his expression unreadable. "You've been avoiding me," he said after a beat.

"I didn't realize I was *obligated* to entertain you," Elizabeth replied, her tone biting.

Paul chuckled, the sound low and deliberate. "You're sharp. *Luc always said that about you.*"

The mention of Luc's name sent a jolt through her. She narrowed her eyes. "How do you know Luc?"

Paul tilted his head, his gaze steady. "Marc and I are colleagues. Luc came to us for... *help.*"

Elizabeth's heart pounded. "*Help?*" she repeated, her voice barely above a whisper.

Paul's smile didn't reach his eyes. "He was struggling. You know that better than anyone. We tried to be there for him, but *some wounds run too deep.*"

The words hung in the air, heavy with implication. Elizabeth's mind raced, piecing together fragments of memory and suspicion. Luc had been private about his struggles, but she'd sensed the weight he carried. Had Paul been part of that hidden chapter of Luc's life? And if so, *why was he here now?*

"Why are you *really* here?" Elizabeth demanded, her voice trembling.

Paul's expression shifted, a flicker of something dark crossing his face. "I could ask you the same question," he said, his tone measured. "You've been isolating yourself, pushing away the people who care about you. *Maybe it's time you faced the truth.*"

Elizabeth took a step back, her pulse racing. *"What truth?"*

Paul's gaze bore into hers. "That you can't keep running from the past. *Luc's gone, Elizabeth. But the questions you're avoiding? They won't disappear.*"

The words struck her like a physical blow. She turned away, unable to meet his eyes. Her breath came in shallow gasps as the walls of her reality seemed to close in. She needed answers, but the fear of what she might uncover paralyzed her.

The dinner table felt suffocating when Elizabeth returned. The conversations around her were fragmented, voices overlapping in a chaotic symphony. Claire and Chloé exchanged cryptic remarks about loss and healing, their words laced with an *unsettling familiarity.* Elizabeth's gaze darted to Marc, who sat at the head of the table, his demeanor calm and composed. He seemed to sense her watching and met her eyes with a steady gaze.

"Are you feeling better?" Marc asked, his tone polite but probing.

Elizabeth nodded, though her throat felt tight. "Just needed some air."

"Air can do wonders," Chloé said, her smile enigmatic. "Especially when the past feels *too heavy to bear.*"

Elizabeth's chest tightened. The way Chloé spoke, as if she knew more than she let on, sent a chill down her spine. She glanced at Claire, who avoided her gaze, and then at Paul, whose expression remained inscrutable.

The room felt *charged with unspoken tension,* each word and glance layered with hidden meaning. Elizabeth's paranoia surged. *Were they all in on something?* Did they know the truth about Luc's death? Or was her mind playing tricks on her again?

Later, as the evening wound down, Elizabeth found herself alone in the library. The dimly lit room was lined with shelves of leather-bound books, their spines gleaming in the soft light. She ran her fingers along the edge of the desk, her thoughts racing.

"You're not imagining it, you know."

The voice startled her, and she turned to see Marc standing in the doorway. He stepped inside, closing the door behind him.

"Not imagining what?" Elizabeth asked, her voice wary.

Marc leaned against the desk, his posture relaxed but his eyes intense. "The feeling that something's off. That there are things you don't know."

Elizabeth's breath caught. "What are you talking about?"

Marc 's gaze didn't waver. "Luc trusted me. He told me things he couldn't tell anyone else. Things about his past, his fears, his regrets."

Elizabeth's heart pounded as Marc 's words sank in. Her breath hitched, and a wave of dread coursed through her. *Luc's death was an accident.* The room seemed to close in around her, the air suddenly too thick to breathe.

"You're lying," she whispered, her voice trembling, though the doubt was painfully clear.

Marc shook his head, his expression heavy with regret. "I wish I were. But you deserve to know the truth, Elizabeth. Even if it's painful."

Her knees threatened to give way, and she gripped the edge of the desk for support, her knuckles white. Marc 's voice faded into the background as a single thought consumed her mind: *Samuel.*

Fumbling for her phone, Elizabeth dialed her son's number with shaking hands. She pressed the device to her ear, her heart hammering in her chest. Each ring felt like an eternity, the panic rising with every unanswered call.

"Pick up, pick up, pick up," she murmured under her breath, her voice cracking with desperation.

The call went to voicemail.

"Samuel, it's Mom," she said, her voice barely steady. "Please call me back as soon as you get this. It's important." She ended the call, her fingers trembling as she tried again.

This time, she texted him: *Samuel, where are you? Please answer me. I need to know you're okay.*

Her mind raced with worst-case scenarios, the fear gnawing at her resolve. She glanced at Marc, who was watching her, his expression unreadable.

"I can't reach him," she said, her voice breaking. "What if something's happened to him too?"

Marc stepped closer, his tone calm but firm. "Elizabeth, take a deep breath. We'll figure this out. Samuel's probably fine."

But his words did little to soothe her. The silence on the other end of the line felt deafening, and the fear that had been simmering beneath the surface now threatened to consume her entirely.

Elizabeth's vision blurred, tears pricking at her eyes. She wanted to scream, to demand answers, but the fear of what Marc might reveal kept her silent. Her mind raced with possibilities, each one more terrifying than the last. *Was Luc's death tied to Paul? To Marc? To something darker than she could comprehend?*

Marc stepped closer, his voice soft but insistent. "You're not alone in this. Whatever you're feeling, whatever you're afraid of, you don't have to face it by yourself."

Elizabeth's chest ached, the weight of her grief and suspicion threatening to crush her. She looked up at Marc, her vision swimming. For a moment, she thought she saw Luc's face, his eyes filled with love and sorrow. Her breath hitched, and she reached out, her fingers brushing against Marc 's hand.

"*Luc?*" she whispered, her voice trembling.

Marc 's expression softened, but he didn't correct her. Instead, he squeezed her hand gently, his touch grounding her. Elizabeth closed her eyes, the lines between past and present blurring. She could almost hear Luc's voice, feel his presence, as if he were standing right beside her.

"*I miss you,*" she murmured, her voice thick with emotion. "*I don't know how to keep going without you.*"

Marc 's grip tightened slightly, his silence speaking volumes. Elizabeth opened her eyes, her gaze meeting his. The illusion shattered, and she saw Marc for who he was. But the vulnerability in his eyes, the quiet understanding, reminded her of Luc in a way that both comforted and unsettled her.

"You're stronger than you think," Marc said softly.

Elizabeth's throat tightened, and she looked away, unable to hold his gaze any longer. The room felt suffocating, the weight of her emotions too much to bear. She pulled her hand back, retreating a step.

CHAPTER 6

THE BREAKING POINT

Elizabeth's breathing came in shallow gasps as she clutched the edge of the vanity in her room. The mirror reflected a pale, drawn version of herself, her eyes wide with a fear she couldn't suppress. She splashed cold water on her face, hoping the shock would pull her from the spiraling thoughts that threatened to consume her. But the *memories*—or were they *hallucinations?*—clung to her mind like cobwebs.

She'd seen *Luc.*

Not in the way she remembered him, vibrant and full of life, but as a *shadow*, a *specter* lingering just beyond her reach. His face had been gaunt, his eyes hollow, and his lips had moved soundlessly, as if trying to warn her of something. Or *someone.*

The knock on her door startled her. Elizabeth turned sharply, her heart hammering in her chest. "Who is it?" she called, her voice trembling.

"It's Claire," came the soft reply. "Can I come in?"

Elizabeth hesitated. Claire's presence had been unsettling lately, her words too measured, her actions too deliberate. But denying her entry would only raise more questions. "Come in," Elizabeth said, her voice barely above a whisper.

Claire entered, her steps light and unhurried. She carried a tray with a steaming cup of tea and a plate of biscuits. "I thought you might need something to help you relax," she said, setting the tray on the bedside table. Her smile was warm, but her eyes held an intensity that made Elizabeth's skin prickle.

"Thank you," Elizabeth murmured, though she made no move to touch the tea. "I'm fine, really. Just a little tired."

Claire sat on the edge of the bed, her gaze never leaving Elizabeth. "You've been through so much, *Lizzie*. It's only natural to feel… *unsteady*. But you don't have to face this alone. *We're* all here for you."

"*We?*" Elizabeth's voice was sharper than she intended, but she couldn't help it. The word felt *loaded*, as though it carried a deeper meaning.

Claire's smile faltered for a fraction of a second before returning. "Me, Chloe, Marc. Even Paul, in his own way. We're all worried about you."

Elizabeth's stomach churned. She wanted to believe Claire, to take comfort in her words, but the nagging doubt in her mind refused to be silenced. "I appreciate it," she said finally, her tone flat. "But I'm fine. Really."

Claire reached out and placed a hand on Elizabeth's arm. Her touch was light, almost comforting, but Elizabeth couldn't shake the feeling of being *trapped*. "If you ever want to talk, you know where to find me," Claire said, her voice soft but firm.

As soon as Claire left, Elizabeth locked the door and leaned against it, her chest heaving. The room felt *suffocating*, the walls closing in. She needed to get out, to clear her head. Grabbing her shawl, she slipped out through the side door and into the garden.

The night air was cool and crisp, the garden bathed in moonlight. Elizabeth wandered aimlessly, her thoughts a tangled mess. The memory of *Luc's face* haunted her, and she couldn't shake the feeling that she was being *watched*.

A rustling sound behind her made her spin around, her heart pounding. Paul emerged from the shadows, his hands tucked casually into his pockets. "Couldn't rest?" he asked, his tone neutral.

Elizabeth crossed her arms, trying to steady herself. "Just needed some air."

Paul studied her for a moment, his gaze penetrating. "You've been on edge all night. Is there something you're not telling us?"

Elizabeth bristled. "I don't know what you mean."

He stepped closer, his expression unreadable. "I think you do. *Luc's death*… it left a lot of unanswered questions. For all of us."

Her breath caught. "What are you saying?"

Paul's eyes narrowed. "I'm saying that maybe it's time we stop pretending everything's fine. You're not the only one who's struggling to make sense of what happened."

Elizabeth's chest tightened. She wanted to scream at him, to demand answers, but the fear of what he might say kept her silent. Instead, she turned and walked away, her footsteps echoing in the stillness.

Back inside, Elizabeth found herself drawn to the library. The room was dimly lit, the scent of old books and polished wood filling the air. She sank into one of the armchairs, her mind racing. Fragments of memories surfaced—*Luc's laughter, his touch, the way he'd looked at her as if she were his entire world.* But those memories were *tainted* now, overshadowed by the image of his lifeless body.

The sound of the door creaking open made her sit up. Marc entered, his expression calm but his eyes shadowed. "Couldn't sleep?" he asked, echoing Paul's earlier words.

Elizabeth shook her head. "Too much on my mind."

Marc sat across from her, his posture relaxed. "That's understandable. Grief has a way of *unraveling* us."

She studied him, searching for any sign of deceit. "Do you think I'm unraveling?"

His lips curved into a faint smile. "I think you're trying to make sense of something senseless. And that's not easy."

Elizabeth's gaze dropped to her hands, which were clenched in her lap. "Sometimes I feel like I'm losing my mind. Like I can't trust what I see or hear."

Marc leaned forward, his expression earnest. "You're not crazy, Elizabeth. You're *grieving*. And grief can make us question everything. But you're stronger than you think."

His words were meant to comfort her, but they only deepened her unease. She wanted to believe him, to take solace in his presence, but the nagging doubt in her mind refused to be silenced.

The dinner party felt like a distant memory by the time Elizabeth returned to her room. She was about to collapse onto the bed when something caught her eye. A leather satchel sat on the desk, partially open. It wasn't hers.

Curiosity and suspicion warred within her. Slowly, she approached the bag and peered inside. Her breath caught when she saw it: *Luc's watch*. The one he'd been wearing the day he died.

Her hands trembled as she reached for it, her mind racing. *Why would Marc have this? What did it mean?*

A knock at the door made her jump. She quickly shoved the watch back into the bag and closed it. "Who is it?" she called, her voice shaky.

"It's Marc," came the reply. "Can we talk?"

Elizabeth's pulse raced. She hesitated, glancing at the bag. "Just a moment," she said, her voice strained.

She needed answers, but the fear of what she might uncover was almost too much to bear. As she opened the door, Marc's concerned expression greeted her, but her mind was elsewhere, consumed by the growing web of *secrets and lies.*

And the terrifying realization that she could trust *no one.*

CHAPTER 7

UNRAVELING THE TRUTH

Elizabeth paced the dimly lit library, her thoughts a tangled web of suspicion and guilt. The weight of Luc's watch in her hand felt unbearable, its familiar ticking an eerie echo of the past. She turned it over, the engraving on the back—*Forever Yours, E*—mocking her. How had it ended up in Marc's bag?

Her mind raced with questions. Marc and Paul knew Luc, but how? The memories of Luc's struggles surfaced, fragmented and painful. He had always been so private, shielding her from his darkest moments. But now, it seemed there was a whole side of him she had never known.

The sound of footsteps broke her reverie. Elizabeth stuffed the watch into her pocket just as Marc entered the room. His calm demeanor only heightened her unease.

"You've been avoiding me," Marc said, his voice measured. He leaned casually against the desk, but his eyes were sharp, watching her every move.

"I've had a lot on my mind," Elizabeth replied, her tone guarded.

Marc nodded, as if he understood more than she was willing to admit. "I imagine finding Luc's watch stirred up some memories."

Elizabeth's breath caught. She hadn't mentioned the watch to anyone. "How did you—"

"Paul told me," Marc interrupted, his expression unreadable. "He saw you with it earlier."

Elizabeth clenched her fists, her pulse quickening. "Why was it in your bag?"

Marc sighed, his shoulders sagging slightly. "It's not what you think. Luc came to me a few months before the accident. He was struggling, Elizabeth. More than you realized."

Her chest tightened. "Struggling with what?"

Marc hesitated, as if weighing how much to reveal. "Luc was dealing with severe depression and anxiety. He sought help from me and Paul. We worked together at the time—at a psychiatric facility."

Elizabeth's mind reeled. "You're a doctor?"

"Yes," Marc admitted. "A psychiatrist. Paul is my colleague, assisting with patient care. Luc came to us voluntarily, but he insisted on keeping it private. He didn't want you to worry."

Elizabeth's legs felt weak, and she sank into a nearby chair. "Why didn't he tell me? I could've helped him."

Marc's expression softened. "He didn't want you to see him that way. He loved you, Elizabeth. He wanted to protect you from his pain."

The words hit her like a blow. She thought back to the months leading up to the accident—the late nights, the distant looks, the unspoken tension. She had chalked it up to stress, never imagining the depth of his struggles.

"What does any of this have to do with the accident?" she asked, her voice trembling.

Marc hesitated again, his gaze dropping to the floor. "Luc's mental state was fragile, but the accident wasn't his fault. Or ours." He looked up, his eyes piercing. "Elizabeth, you were driving that night."

The room spun, and Elizabeth gripped the armrests of the chair. The memories she had buried so deeply clawed their way to the surface—rain-slicked roads, blinding headlights, Luc's voice shouting her name. The impact. The screams.

"No," she whispered, shaking her head. "It wasn't me. It couldn't have been."

Marc stepped closer, his voice gentle but firm. "You've been blaming yourself subconsciously, burying the truth because it's too painful. That's why your mind has been fracturing. The guilt, the grief—it's all been building up."

Tears blurred her vision as the weight of his words settled over her. "I didn't mean to—"

"I know," Marc said softly. "It was an accident. But you need to face the truth if you're ever going to heal."

Elizabeth's heart ached with the enormity of it all. She had spent so long running from the past, convincing herself that someone else was to blame. But deep down, she had always known.

"Why are you telling me this now?" she asked, her voice raw.

Marc hesitated, then reached into his pocket and pulled out a folded piece of paper. He handed it to her without a word.

Elizabeth unfolded it with trembling hands. It was a letter, written in Luc's familiar handwriting.

Elizabeth,

If you're reading this, it means I couldn't find the strength to tell you in person. I've been struggling for a long time, and I know I've kept too much from you. Please don't blame yourself for what happened. You've always been my light, even in my darkest moments.

I sought help because I wanted to be better for you, for us. Marc and Paul tried to help me, but some battles are too big to fight alone. I'm sorry I didn't let you in. Please forgive me.

Love always, Luc.

The letter slipped from her hands as sobs wracked her body. Marc knelt beside her, his presence steady and grounding.

"I didn't want you to find out this way," he said quietly. "But you deserve to know the truth."

Elizabeth wiped her tears, her mind a whirlwind of emotions. "Why did you keep this from me?"

"Luc asked me to," Marc admitted. "He wanted to protect you, even after he was gone."

Elizabeth's chest tightened with a mix of love and anger. Luc had always been so selfless, even to his own detriment. But his secrets had left her adrift, struggling to make sense of a world without him.

"What about Paul?" she asked, her voice steadier now. "Why is he here?"

"Paul came to support me," Marc explained. "When he heard you were struggling, he thought he could help. He's been worried about you, Elizabeth. We both have."

Elizabeth's mind churned with conflicting emotions. She didn't know whether to feel grateful or betrayed. But one thing was clear—she couldn't keep running from the past.

"I need time," she said finally, her voice firm despite the tears still streaming down her face. "Time to process everything."

Marc nodded, his expression understanding. "Take all the time you need. Just know that you're not alone in this."

Elizabeth stood, the weight of Luc's watch in her pocket grounding her. She looked at Marc, then at the letter on the floor. The truth was painful, but it was a start. A step toward healing.

As she left the library, her mind was still heavy with questions. But for the first time in a long time, she felt a glimmer of hope. The path ahead would be difficult, but she was ready to face it—one step at a time.

CHAPTER 8

THE FINAL DINNER

The dining room was cloaked in an eerie stillness, broken only by the faint clinking of silverware against porcelain. Elizabeth sat at the head of the table, her eyes darting between Marc and Paul. The weight of their gazes felt suffocating, as though they were *dissecting her thoughts, peeling back layers she wasn't ready to expose.* The table was set immaculately, but the atmosphere was anything but inviting. Each bite of food tasted like *ash,* every sip of wine a *struggle to swallow.*

"You've been quiet tonight, Elizabeth," Marc said, his voice low and measured. His calm demeanor only added to her unease.

"Just tired," she replied, forcing a smile that didn't reach her eyes.

"Tired or troubled?" Paul interjected, leaning forward slightly. His tone was softer, but it carried an edge of curiosity that made Elizabeth's skin crawl.

She clenched her fists beneath the table, nails digging into her palms. "Why would I be troubled?" she countered, her voice sharper than she intended.

Paul and Marc exchanged a glance, a silent conversation passing between them. Elizabeth's pulse quickened. She had seen *that look* before, the unspoken understanding that made her feel like an outsider in her own life.

The room seemed to close in around her, the walls pressing inward. She felt the *ghost of Luc's touch* on her shoulder, the *echo of his voice* whispering her name. Her chest tightened as fragments of memory and hallucination blurred together. The line between *reality and illusion* had become a frayed thread, threatening to snap.

"You've been remembering things, haven't you?" Marc's question was gentle, but it struck her like a *blow*.

Elizabeth's breath hitched. "What do you mean?"

"Luc," he said simply. The name hung in the air like a *curse*.

Her fork clattered onto her plate, the sound echoing unnaturally loud in the oppressive silence. "Why do you keep bringing him up?" she demanded, her voice trembling. "Why can't you just let him rest?"

"Because you can't," Paul said, his gaze piercing. "And until you do, you'll *never* find peace."

Elizabeth pushed back her chair, the legs scraping against the floor. "I don't have to listen to this," she snapped, rising to her feet. But as she turned to leave, Marc's voice stopped her cold.

"Samuel."

She froze, her heart pounding in her chest. Slowly, she turned back to face them. "What did you say?"

Marc's expression was unreadable. "Your son. *Samuel.* You've been seeing him, haven't you?"

Tears welled in Elizabeth's eyes, but she refused to let them fall. "He's alive," she said, her voice barely above a whisper. "He's at a friend's house. He's *safe.*"

Paul shook his head, his expression filled with something that looked like pity. "Elizabeth, you know that's not true."

"Stop it," she said, her voice rising. "You don't know *anything* about my son."

"We know more than you think," Marc said. "And deep down, so do you."

The room spun around her as memories surged to the surface, unbidden and relentless. The *screech of tires*, the *shattering of glass*, the *deafening silence* that followed. And then Samuel's laughter, so vivid and real it made her heart ache. But the laughter faded, replaced by the *cold, hard truth* she had buried beneath layers of denial.

"No," she whispered, shaking her head. "No, he's alive. He has to be."

"Elizabeth," Paul said gently, "Samuel was in the car with Luc and you. You were driving, I'm sorry. But... I'm afraid he didn't make it."

Her knees buckled, and she sank back into her chair. The room blurred as tears streamed down her face. "Why didn't anyone tell me?" she cried. "Why did you let me believe he was alive?"

"We didn't," Marc said. "You did. Your mind created a version of reality where Samuel survived because the truth was *too much to bear*."

Elizabeth's sobs wracked her body as the weight of their words settled over her. The memories she had clung to, the visions of Samuel, had all been *lies she told herself* to escape the unbearable pain of losing him.

But as the grief threatened to consume her, another memory surfaced—one she had buried even deeper. The argument with Luc, his cruel words cutting into her like *knives*. The *blinding rage* that had consumed her as she gripped the steering wheel. And the moment of clarity, too late, when she realized Samuel was in the backseat.

"Oh, God," she whispered, her voice trembling. "It was my fault."

Marc and Paul exchanged a glance, their expressions grim. "What do you mean?" Paul asked cautiously.

Elizabeth's breath came in shallow gasps as the truth clawed its way to the surface. "I caused the accident," she admitted, her voice barely audible. "I was so angry at Luc, I wasn't thinking clearly. I knew Samuel was in the car, but I didn't think it would go *that* far..."

The room fell silent, the weight of her confession hanging heavily in the air. Marc and Paul said nothing, their faces a mix of shock and sorrow.

Elizabeth buried her face in her hands, her sobs muffled. The truth was out, and there was no escaping it. She had killed her husband and her son, and no amount of denial or delusion could change that.

When she finally looked up, Marc and Paul were gone. The dining room was empty, the table bare. She was alone, just as she had been all along.

The walls of the room dissolved, revealing the *sterile white* of the institution. The dinner party, Marc, Paul—all of it had been a *construct of her fractured mind.* She sat in a padded chair, her arms wrapped tightly around herself.

"Elizabeth," a voice called softly. She looked up to see a nurse standing in the doorway, her expression kind but cautious. "It's time for your medication."

Elizabeth nodded numbly, her mind a whirlwind of memories and revelations. As the nurse approached, she glanced at the empty chair across from her. For a moment, she thought she saw Samuel sitting there, his *bright eyes and innocent smile* filling her with a bittersweet ache.

But when she blinked, he was gone.

The nurse handed her a small cup of pills and a glass of water. Elizabeth took them without protest, swallowing the *bitter truth* along with the medication. She leaned back in her chair, staring at the ceiling as tears slid silently down her cheeks.

In the quiet of the institution, Elizabeth finally faced the truth she had been running from. The accident, the loss, the guilt—it was all hers to bear. And as the weight of it settled over her, she realized that the only person she needed to forgive was *herself.*

Liz's chest tightened as the memory surged back—the accident, Samuel's screams piercing through the chaos. Her rage had consumed her that day, blinding her to the red light and the precious life in the back seat. The therapist's voice pulled her from the abyss, but the guilt lingered, suffocating her. Across the room, Claire avoided her gaze, her own pain etched into her features, while Chloe's sharp voice broke the silence. They were braced by belts on to their own beds, they were soldiers of war and had now become delirious because of repeated trauma and were now suffering from PTSD.

"We all have our ghosts. The question is, will we face them?"

But forgiveness would not come easily. Not tonight. *Perhaps not ever.*